A CHILDHOOD

BOOKS BY TEO SAVORY

FICTION

Landscape of Dreams, *New York,* 1960
The Single Secret, *New York,* 1961; *London,* 1962
A Penny For The Guy, *London,* 1963; *New York,* 1964
To A High Place, *Santa Barbara,* 1972
A Clutch of Fables, *Greensboro,* 1977
Stonecrop: The Country I Remember, *Greensboro,* 1977
A Childhood, *Greensboro,* 1978

POETRY

Traveler's Palm, 1967
Snow Vole, 1968
Transitions, 1973
Dragons of Mist and Torrent, 1974

TRANSLATIONS

ELEVEN VISITATIONS, katrina von hutten, *Munich,* 1971
(with Ursula Mahlendorf) THE CELL, Horst Bienek, *Santa Barbara*
and *Toronto,* 1972; *London,* 1974
SELECTED POEMS, Guillevic, *London* and *Baltimore,* 1973
EUCLIDIANS Guillevic, *Greensboro,* 1975
(with Vo-Dinh) ZEN POEMS, Nhat Hanh, *Greensboro,* 1976

FOR THE UNICORN FRENCH SERIES

Supervielle, 1967
Corbière, 1967
Michaux, 1967
Queneau, 1971

Prévert 1, 1967
Jammes, 1967
Prévert II, 1967
Guillevic, 1968

FOR THE UNICORN GERMAN SERIES

Günter Eich, 1971

A
CHILD

Teo Savory

HOOD

Unicorn Press

ISBN 0-87775-123-4, cloth
ISBN 0-87775-124-2, paper

UNICORN PRESS, INC.

Post Office Box 3307

Greensboro, North Carolina 27402

LIBRARY OF CONGRESS CATALOGING IN PUBLICATION DATA

Savory, Teo.
  A Childhood.

  I. Title.
PZ4.S268Ch   (PS3569.A85)   813'.5'4   78-8912

for my friends

E.A. & G.A.

A
Childhood

I
Arriving

Mother and Nickie are sitting at the dining table, doing Nickie's home work. Also they are talking about me. "Sun," Mother is saying, "he used to look at it till he was dazzled."

I draw a big sun in the sky looking down on our hill.

"It was the first word he could say."

Father told me the first word I could say was "Father". But I do not tell them that. It is better to keep quiet and go on with my drawing.

"He used to cry to go out when the sun was shining on the snow."

"Then we had to push that old buggy up that slippery hill," Nickie says.

I remember it was cold outside. Mother pushed, Nickie walked beside us. The sun was brighter out there. "Let *me* push him." Then when we got to the top of the hill Nickie gave a big push and let go. I was going down the hill very fast with the sun streaking after. Then I couldn't see the sun. My face was in the snow and it hurt. Mother picked me up and put me under her coat where it was warm and soft. Nickie was crying. When Father came home, she cried some more. Father tossed me high in the air and caught me again. "Throw me, too," Nickie said, but he went outside without answering. Then it was night, when things used to come out of the dark corners of our bedroom and make me cry. Nickie got up and came over to my bed. But instead of giving me my soft rabbit and tucking in my blanket, she pinched me and said, *"Baby."*

All that was a long time ago and now I am five years old and know my own name and how to get dressed by myself and tie up my shoes. My sister is eight years old and goes to school every morning on the school bus and when it's winter she does not come home till the sun has started to go behind the mountain. But this year I will go to school the same as she does. My sister's name is Nicolette but everyone calls her Nickie except Mother. Mother calls her My Little Princess. My name is the same as my father's, Jean-Louis Gautier. But everyone except Father calls me Johnny. My father says our name one way, everybody else another. I like his way. But it doesn't matter because everybody in Stonecrop calls him Frenchy. I can say my name exactly the way he does, but I only do that when I'm alone, or alone with him. Otherwise, when someone asks me, I say, "Johnny *Go*-shee," as they expect me to. Nickie says she does not like our name, but she hasn't told me why.

Now Mother has gone in the kitchen and I have finished drawing the sun following me down the hill into the snow. I lie down on the rug in front of the fireplace where Champion is lying and I tell him about going to school. "We go on the school bus, it's yellow. All the cars on the road have to stop when it stops. We take our lunch with us and when we come home we'll get milk and cookies." Nickie sneaks up and pokes Champion with her foot.

"You stupid baby, don't you know you can't take a big stupid dog to school?" She pokes him again.

"Leave him alone, he's *my* dog." Nickie says *she* doesn't want him. "Leave him alone, then. Father gave him to me and he's mine."

She goes and makes a fuss over Slugger, but Slugger's not her cat, he's nobody's. He just came here. She tries to pet him and he gives her a bat with his paw.

"Slugger doesn't want to be petted. Stupid yourself."

"Baby! Anybody knows you don't take a dog to school. Anyhow, you aren't going to school, you're only going to kindergarten with the other babies." Then she looks at me and says, "*Cry*-baby."

Now I do not want to go to school. When Father comes home I do not want to be tossed in the air. "The dog, he will take you to the school bus and be waiting there when you come 'ome," my father says. "And you will have a new snow-suit."

"It's still summer, what's all the fuss?" Mother says.

It is warm outdoors, not night yet or even dark, so I run out and look to see if my toad is still under the tomato plants.

He's there all right. I see his tongue flick out like a fork of lightning and then all in one second he's caught a mosquito and eaten it. He lets me stroke him on the head. Nickie says touching frogs or toads will give you warts. I *want* warts. I look and look but I do not get even one. Only a little slime from the toad's head.

In the morning the grass is white and the tomato plants are black and so are Mother's dahlias. It is frost.

"Summer is over," Mother says. She hugs herself with her own arms and then she puts on her fuzzy blue sweater. One leaf falls on the frosted grass by my feet. I look at it. It is not really red, not like the red crayon in my box, and it isn't like the orange crayon either. What is it, then? I look at all its different colors and at the veins strong as twigs and at its pointed ends, and even when Mother calls me to come and put my jacket on I still look. Then I pick it up and take it into my room and put it away with my other things.

II
Winter

Cold waiting for the school bus. We run out of the house, I am always first, Nickie last. Mother stands in the doorway only one minute, rubbing her arms underneath the sleeves of her fuzzy blue sweater. "Johnny, Johnny, come back, you forgot your . . ." But I don't go back. Let Nickie go back. Sometimes she does, sometimes not. If she doesn't then sometimes I don't have my mittens. Then I put my lunch box under one arm and my crayon box under the other arm and put my hands in the pockets of my snowsuit. But you can't do that all the time because there are often things to pick up . . . I run all the way down our path to our driveway. Champion runs with me. He runs twice as far as I do because he runs ahead a few feet, then back again, all along the way. Our car isn't in our turn-around. Father went to work at daylight. There's a black grease spot on the snow, and the snow is all churned up from the wheels spinning and spinning because the car was too cold to start. Champion makes a big yellow spot beside the black spot and his spot steams. I remember the noise the engine made at daylight, but I was in bed, my head under the covers until Nickie pulled them off.

I run up Bradford Road to the corner of the Afton Road. That's where Nickie catches up. Sometimes she hits me with her book bag. But I don't care: I got here first. But sometimes, if I forget my mittens, she gives me one of hers, then we each have one warm hand and one cold one. It's time for Champion to go home now. He doesn't run when he has to go back. We stamp our feet while we wait for the bus but we get cold anyhow. The tip of Nickie's nose gets red. "The tip of your nose is red." — "*Your* nose is red all over." Mrs. Ambler's cat comes out, that big she-cat that fights with Slugger. I can see all the way up the Amblers' driveway the other side of Bradford Road from our corner. The peony bushes are under the snow. The cat sniffs the air. It runs back in the house before I can get a snowball ready. Nickie says "Don't," anyhow. Here comes our big yellow bus. The driver

9

is my friend and he is named Fred and he's grouchy because he has to get his own breakfast (Mother says). We're the first ones. I run up and down the aisle. "Sit down or Fred will report you." But he never does. The bus stops, starts, a thousand times. It gets full. I sit beside Nickie, whether she wants me to or not. Most of those boys are *big*. They make noise. The bus is filled with noise. Nickie whispers to her girl friends in the seat behind, but they can't hear each other. I sit still. Then we're at school.

When we get home the afternoon is going away behind the mountain, so early because it's winter. Champion's waiting at the bus stop. First he runs around us in a circle barking, then he jumps on me and knocks me over and licks my face. His tongue is big and scratchy. "Come on quick. We got to get the sled out before it's too dark . . ." Nickie's already running home, calling to me over her shoulder. The snow is firm and smooth on the hill behind our house. The sled leaves tracks like knife cuts. "Why didn't you wait till Christmas?" Mother said when Father brought it home. "You spoil him," she said. "The girl, she can ride it too," Father said, in his voice that is always different. "And the snow, it is now," he said, "Christmas, it is later." So we can pull the sled to the top of the hill and coast down. But it is not coasting. It is flying. Those men flying around in the air in my picture book don't fly any more than I do on our sled. We pull up hill and then fly down, over and over, till Mother calls, "Come in," out the back window. "One more time . . ." Champion runs beside us. I am sorry *he* cannot fly. "Johnny . . . Nickie . . ." — "One more time . . ." We bump a rock and turn over. I roll and roll. The snow is light and fluffy and inside my neckband and cuffbands, my waistband and the edge of my cap it is cold and it tickles. I roll and roll. I am in the snow. I *am* snow.

Happy.

"Come on, it's almost dark." Nickie tickles my stomach and laughs. I pull her arm. We roll in the snow. We run up the hill and roll down it: *we* are the sled. Snow, and rolling and rolling. Laughing. Champion barking. Happy.

"I'll tell your father . . ." Mother's in front of the television set, rubbing her arms. "You're making puddles on my clean floor. Look at your snowsuits. I'll tell your father."

"Snowsuits are for snow," Nickie says. Fresh. Mother scolds. Then Nickie gets different, she looks mean. "It's *his* fault, he knocked me down." I'll put a snake in her bed for that. But it's winter and I haven't got a snake. Even my toad is gone. Winter is only snow.

"Liar." We're in our room. "Liar," I say. She cries when I hit her. Mother comes in and slaps me. Now everybody can stay in our room and cry.

When Father comes in it is dark. His face will be red and purple all over from working outdoors. His fingers will be red, too, and twice as big as they were at breakfast. Champion and Slugger are lying in front of the fireplace, stretched out. There's not even one inch for Father. He gives them each a boot. "They eat. They do nothing. They pay no taxes." His voice is rough. "Then they give me no fire." Slugger runs down cellar and Champion gets under the table. Then Father turns off the television set. He calls to Mother: "You the same."

I run out to him. He picks me up. He looks at my face. "You good boy?" "In the sled, Father . . ." He tosses me in the air, saying, "Jean, Jean, Jean-*nee*," over and over, like singing and his voice is not rough. He always catches me.

Mother hurries out of our room. "He's bad. He hit Nickie." Father gives me one on the ear. Then he asks Mother: "What *she* do?"

I go back in our room because Father and Mother are talking to each other. Pretty soon he's going to soak his hands and face slowly so they won't get frost bite, then he will wash the lime dust off himself. Then he will want his supper and I do not smell any soup. Maybe Mother was watching the television and forgot again? So I do not go in the bathroom and watch Father get clean and watch him shave and brush his black hair and put the oil on it that smells of violets. My hair is black, too, but he puts water on mine — until I am older, he says. But tonight I stay in our bedroom. If Mother forgot the soup again he will tell her about lazy Irish and that she does nothing and pays no taxes, and maybe he will even take the insides out of the television set but this time he would not smash them because that costs forty dollars.

So I stay in our room with Nickie. She still looks mean but after while she doesn't, and while Father and Mother are talking she shows me all the shells she got from Auntie Loretta and the beads Grandma sent her from Lourdes. Now I will show her my dried plants and my snake's skin.

The creek froze over a long time ago, but now there is ice everywhere. On our back steps and on the windshield of Father's car. Father has to chop ice off the steps and path every morning and he goes to work in Mr. Ambler's car. Slugger lies by the fire and won't go out. Champion doesn't stay out long. We cannot get to the Afton road, so even if it wasn't Christmas vacation we wouldn't be able to go to school. Too bad the ice doesn't come while school is open. But Mother says I must go to school so that I can go to college. Mother and Nickie sew or look at television. I look at the icicles on the windows: they are different shapes and inside of each one are many different colors. My crayons don't know those colors, so I cannot draw. I wish I could go out. Mother wishes she was in the Bronx. She cries. When Father comes home he can't say anything because his lips are frozen. He does not toss me in the air and even when his lips are thawed out, along with his hands and feet, he doesn't talk. In the night once I heard Mother crying and then I heard Father talking.

The quarry is closing down because of the ice and Mother says we will have no Christmas. Father says he is *making* our Christmas. He goes with Mr. Ambler to Stonecrop (Mother says she is not going out in the ice), he goes to the store for her and to the hardware store for himself. The rest of the day he's in the attic, sawing and hammering. Mother wanted to go to the Bronx for Christmas to visit Auntie Loretta, but Father says the car won't start and we have no money and anyhow families should stay home for Christmas.

I ask Nickie what is the Bronx. "Stupid, it's New York City." But what is that? "It's where I was born," she says. "Why were you born there and I wasn't?" She says because that's where Mother and Father lived then. "You were there, once," she says, "but I guess you don't remember." She tells me about streets with stores and buses, and lots of people sitting in a park and lots of different families living in one house, and movies and supermarkets. "Better than here in the backwoods," she says. I think it sounds awful. Also I do not think she remembers any of those things she talks about, they're only what Mother *told* her. But I decide not to say so.

Now it is Christmas and the ice is melting and the quarry will open soon. No one is silent or crying any more and this morning Father took me up to the attic and showed me my room he is building. It will be mine starting next summer, as soon as it's warm. Not now because there's no heat and Father can't put that in till the furnace is turned off. There's a new floor and walls all covered with boards and a closet and a bed built over a chest of drawers like a bunk on a ship. There's a big window and from it I can see the top of our hill and then down it past Mrs. Bradford's cottage to where the ice shines on the frozen creek. Beyond that is the mountain, covered with snow and bare trees that will get green again in the spring. My bunk is under the window. Father says now that it isn't a surprise any more I can help him finish the walls and nail on the baseboards. Soon, when he gets back to work again, I will have my own toolbox and learn how to use tools like a man.

Father also made a doll's house for Nickie and a workbox for Mother's sewing. The top of the box is different kinds of wood in a pattern.

I guess it was cold working up there but Father said he did not notice.

We had a big turkey and a plum pudding and I had some of Father's wine and got the gold ring out of the pudding that Nickie wanted, so I gave it to her. Afterwards I threw up all over my bed. Nickie said she won't sleep in the same room with a pig. But after winter is over she won't have to.

Fresh snow fell on the melted ice. It was not soft flakes but little shiny pinheads and scrunched under my feet. Champion and I could go out. I had to bundle up but he didn't. We crunched and crunched up our hill. He made his yellow steam-spot. I made a yellow pattern — first like a maple leaf, then like an icicle, and then great big writing. I made writing up and down our whole hillside. I bet I could write over the whole mountain if I went up there. Then I did up my pants and Champion and I ran home.

Nickie went outside and she saw my writing. She ran right back inside to where I was drinking cocoa with Mother, "Johnny peed on the snow."

Mother shut me in the cellar. Father came home. "Jean, Jean, Jean-*nee?*" I heard him because I was sitting on the top step but I didn't answer.

"He's bad, bad and filthy."

"What he do?"

"He urinated on the snow. You must give him a whipping."

Father laughed. "He's a boy!" He let me out of the cellar. Mother and Nickie looked at me with their eyes all squinty. Father put his arm around me. "Why you not liking what is natural, eh?" he asked Mother. "You a woman — or some little *vièrge* like Nickie? Eh?"

"He's just like you. A filthy beast."

Nickie kicked my ankle and said "Filthy beast" too. Father gave her one on the ear.

Nickie forgot I was a filthy beast and I forgot she was a sneak, because we were in our room without any supper and Father and Mother were out in the kitchen hollering at each other. Nickie sat on the side of my bed and read to me. Finally Mother came in with our bowls of soup and some bread. She had big puffy eyelids and a red mark on one side of her face. She didn't say anything and went right out again. But it was quiet out there after that. I was tired of Nickie's reading. She always reads me girls' books instead of my books, so I told her she could tell me some more about the Bronx and pretty soon I went to sleep.

When we got home from school Mother was dressed up, no television, tea on the table, and the priest was there. He took me in our room, but without Nickie, just the two of us, and talked to me. He told me about bad, dirty things and how they hurt the heart of Jesus. He said they also hurt my mother. He said I did not want to be a bad, dirty boy and hurt the heart of Jesus and the heart of His mother, or *my* mother's either, and then he asked me my catechism and told me to learn more. Afterwards we had tea and he blessed us and went away. When Father came home I did not want to be tossed in the air or anything. I went down cellar. Champion wouldn't come so I went alone. Pretty soon Slugger came because he likes it down there. I sat on the bottom step and looked at Slugger and he sat on the next step and looked at me. Every once in a while the furnace would go on with a loud grumble and show its fiery teeth through its window-face, like a Hallowe'en pumpkin, and we would look at it.

I remember when Slugger came to our back door: only one eye, half his tail gone and a scar the whole way round his middle. "What an awful looking creature!" Mother said. She put milk out for him. He waited every morning. Then he sat on the back step all day. At night he went back in the bushes someplace. It was winter then, too. Mother put on her heavy coat and her snow boots and walked all over asking where his home was. Mrs. Ambler didn't know. Mrs. Bradford said, "I seen that nasty Tom hanging around and I give him the broom." The Ballatos had never seen him. Nobody knew where his home was. So Mother told him to come in.

Now I can see that his eye is full of yellow stuff, oozy and smelly. It's the only eye he's got. I would pet him but he won't let me. Anyone pets him, he puts out his big paw and gives you one. Not with his claws out, just a big bat. Even Father. When he used to live on our back step he used to give everybody one on the ankle as they went by, and you can bet that made Father mad.

"Johnny, Johnny. Supper."

I go upstairs and everybody's eating their soup. "Slugger's eye's got pus and it stinks."

"Johnny! And not at the table."

"But his eye's *sick*."

"Then he must go to the vet," Mother says.

"No. He old, sick cat, no use to anyone. I no spend the money."

"Then I'll spend my Christmas money from Loretta."

Father banged on the table and the soup slopped over.

I began to cry. Nickie pinched me. "Baby," she whispered.

Mother sat up straight. "You stop that," she said to Father. "You, too, Johnny. Everybody eat their supper."

Next day Mrs. Ambler took Mother and Slugger to the vet and when they came home Slugger had some yellow ointment to put in his yellow eye and only Mother could put it in without getting his claws.

So much snow fell down in the night that Father could not find the car. He came back in the house and got my Brownie camera and took a picture of a great big snow mound which is where the car was last night. It was bad because he had to get a lift from Mr. Ambler and be late to work again. But good because we could not get to the bus stop and I did not have to sit in school all day. Nickie and Mother and I had breakfast in our pajamas in front of the fire and watched television. It was like being sick or a special holiday. When the sun came out Nickie and I could not take the sled up the hill because the snow was too deep. We made a snowman in front of the house. It is the biggest snowman anyone ever made. When Father came home he wasn't red, he was more like blue, but he tossed me higher than ever and said, "Biggest damn snowman . . ." There was a lot of good hot soup.

In the morning Father got the hose out of the cellar and hooked it up and sprayed the snowman with water so that it will freeze and last longer. Now it is an iceman.

Tonight Father gave me a parcel and said, "Now you can walk on the snow." Snowshoes! Stuff like flat strings weaves back and forth, holding the frames together. They are good to look at, the way frost patterns on the window are, or the veins in a leaf I found once. "You spoil him . . ." Father had another parcel. "*Voilà!* for the girl also." But Nickie does not want snowshoes. She wants dancing-shoes. She cried. Father banged on the dining table again.

But he has given Mother money and Nickie has stopped crying.

Father has a bandage over one eye. A piece of rock from the machine he works in flew up and hit him in the eye. Is it dangerous? Mother said he should get a better job and not be a laborer all his life, but Father said, "I put on a white shirt, I no get so much salary. And what am I knowing? I put on the French Navy blue, that I know very well, but you not like that." I do not know what they are talking about, so I go in our room to try on my snowshoes. Nickie's snowshoes are in the hall closet.

Soon it is Saturday: no school. Our hill is very high because of the snow. But the sun is shining and makes me warm. In my snowshoes I can walk like a giant. I can walk even where Champion can't. I walk to the very top of our hill. The whole world is white. Mr. Ambler's corn field is white and the road is white, and the cottage where Mrs. Bradford lives. I am all alone on top of a white mountain and all around me is white with no marks or tracks. It is my white. I am up very high and I like it. After while I go home to sit in front of the fire and drink hot cocoa.

III
Summer

Summer goes on and on. There is light all the time. When I wake up I see from the window over my bunk that the sun is already awake. Or, sometimes, it is raining and the next day I see that the green things in the garden have grown faster. When Father comes home now it is still day and he is not red or frozen. As soon as he washes off the lime dust we can go outdoors together. We go down to the creek to get our ducks. Mrs. Bradford is angry because, she says, it is her creek, even though my father has explained to her that ducks do not understand about boundary lines. But since the eggs hatched and the little fluffy ones can walk, Mrs. Bradford watches them follow their mothers down the road and into the water, and I saw her laugh. I can see our ducks swimming because I fish off the bridge. I can fish all day if I want to. Or I can go hunting for things up-creek. the side that doesn't belong to Mrs. Bradford, where I found my toad again. I also found a turtle. I bring all my things home and they live at the edge of the vegetable garden near the spring. The beans in the garden are mine because I planted them. Now I must weed them.

Every day I help my father. Even if I am busy fishing I run home when I hear the four o'clock whistle from the quarry. Then I see Father drive up, his face and hair and clothes white with limedust. Last week he chopped down a tree to make into logs and then he could teach me to use the bucksaw with him. This week we are building a better house for the ducks. "Summer, it is so short here," Father says, "one must already start to make ready for the winter." I do not know what he means. He tells me about his day on l'Île d'Oleron when he was a boy — he tells me over and over how to say the name, so that I can say it the way he does, as I can say my own. He tells me how there was more daylight in winter and hardly any snow, no mountains, just the ocean with a lighthouse on it and maybe some windwills, and the beach, miles of sand with things to eat in it that boys could dig

up. "I want to see it, Father." "Some day," he says. I like it
here and I would not want to leave Champion and my toads
and all my things. But I would like to go to Father's beach —
some day . . .

"Let's go fishing, Father." *He* doesn't fish with a worm on
a piece of string. We all go to watch him, even Mother.
Father casts his rod high, the line whistles in the air so fast
you can't see it, lands gently on the water, a fly that he's
made floats there, it floats about one minute before the reel
goes *whee* and the line goes tearing up the creek. Mrs. Bradford leans over her fence. "You'll get fouled in the trees,"
and she laughs. But Father brings in the line and there's a
fish. I know how to tap it on the head and put it in the
basket lined with the ferns I picked on the way. Then Father
casts again, the rod whirls over his head. Every cast, one fish.
We have trout for dinner. Mother won't clean them. So
Father and I sit on the back step and do it.

Then he and I pick strawberries and cut some asparagus.
Dinner is good. "French asparagus," Father says.

"It's no different from what I used to buy in the Bronx."

"Did it grow there on those streets?" I ask her, but she
does not tell me because she's busy talking to Father.

In the morning Father cuts all the asparagus and takes it
into Afton. When he comes home he has a lot of money and
he puts it on the table beside the television set and says, "For
French asparagus. Is not like lazy Irish Bronx asparagus."

Nickie and I go out and go to the Amblers' because Mrs.
Ambler has a new baby. Last year she had new kittens. I
don't care much for the baby, either. Champion can't come in
there. So afterwards I take him up the mountain on a run. We
run up high past marble shelves and little springs and ferns
and mayflower and jack-in-the-pulpits. At the top I can't
run any more and I stop beside a spring. I'm all sweaty and
Champion's tongue hangs out. We drink from the spring. I
can't get enough, lapping with my tongue, so I use my hands.
We both lie down and look at the sky. First there are the tall
ferns with gold spots on their backs, then some bushes in a

tangle — I don't care about them. Then there are the tree
branches of all different shapes and with different shapes to
their leaves. Through them I see the sky, a lot higher.
Look up: shapes of leaves, then sky. Look down: shadows of
leaves, then ground. What I'm lying on is soft. It is moss with
little dots like flowers on it. I take some for Mother. (Not
allowed to pick real flowers up here.) "Come on, Champion."

When I get home I take my crayons out and I draw and
draw. I keep one. I get Nickie from the living room. "Write
on it, Nickie. At the top. Write 'Shady'."

"Baby." She looks: "What a mess." I don't care. I like it.
Mother and Father come in, they must have gone to Stonecrop to the store. I left the moss on the kitchen table. I forgot
it. "What's this mess?" Mother asks. That moss got dry and
crumbled up. I don't like it any more so I throw it out.
"Mother, when I came by Mrs. Bradford's house I saw her
drive away in a car with somebody and her house is all
shut up."

"She rented the place for the summer," Mother says.
"She's gone to Afton to stay with her daughter-in-law. These
Yankees will do anything for money."

"To make rent from the property, that is good."

"Yankees, French peasants, what's the difference?"

"Who's coming there, Mother?"

"The Irish peasants, they are living with the pigs."

"Some city people, Johnny, for the summer."

"Maybe they come from your Bronx, eh? You make
friends, maybe?"

"I'm hungry." I look in the paper sacks. "I want some
milk." Maybe they'll go on talking forever and I'll starve.
"*Milk*."

They stop because there's that cawing outside. Father
runs for his shotgun. "The blue-*jays!*" — he says the "j" his
way, like when he's saying "Jean". He runs outside. "They
eat my ducks' food and they do no*thing*."

Mother begins to laugh. "They pay no tax*es*," she says in
his way. Pop, pop, pop, goes the gun. Father comes to the

back step. He has three bluejays. "We eat him," he says.

"Them," Mother says. "Not him, them. And *I* won't. Only savages eat bluejays," She puts away groceries and finally remembers to give me some milk. Father sits on the back step, pulling feathers out of bluejays. Mother calls Nickie. "Little princess," she calls, " I brought some cookies." I grab one and go out to Father. Those bluejays look funny now, with all their feathers off. Small and naked but still blue. Father looks at them and gets mad. "They are nothing but *'ead*," he says. He throws them at Champion. "*You* eat him," he says. But even Champion doesn't want those bluejays.

The new people came to Mrs. Bradford's house. I was on the bridge fishing. I saw them drive up. I don't know what kind of car that is. They have lots of new suitcases and two old, black cases. The old ones are funny — big and curved at one end, long and thin at the other. I watch from the bridge but pretend not to. *She's* pretty, prettier than Nickie's old Eleanor doll, the whitest skin, whiter than Mother's, and hair the color of a gold maple leaf in the fall. Only she's kind of skinny with narrow legs and such little feet — how can she walk on them? But she does. While the man carries all those suitcases inside she carries the two worn-out black ones, one at a time, in her arms the way Mrs. Ambler carries her baby. Second trip, she sees me and calls out, "Hello, little boy." Who's she calling a little boy? I have my own toolbox now, I hammered all the nails into the baseboards of my own room, and besides I just caught a fish. So I pretend not to hear. Then she says, "It must be a little French boy," and she rattles off something in Father's language.

As soon as they're in the house with the door shut Champion and I run home. I put my fish on the kitchen table. "Mother! I caught a fish! And the new people came."

"What're they like?"

"Mother, why would anybody think I'm a little French boy?"

She comes out to the kitchen and gives me a squinty look.

"I guess you *are* the spitting image of *him*." But she doesn't sound glad about it.

"Mother, look! My fish!"

"Take that thing off my table and take it outside."

I sit on the back step with Slugger and clean my fish, the way Father does, with my new clasp-knife. But it doesn't come out the way Father's do. What a mess. It's only a shiner, anyhow. Slugger can have it. Mother's at the screen-door asking about the new people. But I don't feel like talking. I'd rather look at my toad. So I go and look at my toad. I still haven't got any warts yet.

Mother talks and talks about the new people. She talks to Mrs. Ambler on the telephone. "They're both musicians," she tells Father at supper. "He plays the violin and she plays the piano. She had two crates of china and a grand piano moved in there today."

"I *saw* that," I say. "I didn't have to go quack-quack on the telephone to find out."

"Fresh."

"Well, I did."

"*Tais-toi*, Jean-nee."

That means shut up, or else.

"He's going to teach up at the Center this summer," Mother says, "and play first violin with the Festival Orchestra." Then she asks me again what they look like.

"Why you not going to see for yourself?" Father asks her.

"Oh, I couldn't."

Right away the letter came. Mother says it's an invitation. She says it's addressed to Mr. and Mrs. Jean-Louis Gautier and she reads it out loud at supper. " '. . . Some music, and to meet our neighbors . . . Please come and bring your children.' "

"*She* know about *you*, too, eh?" Father winks at me. "Now you see for yourself."

"Oh, I couldn't. A party . . . Nickie and I have nothing to wear."

"*Jésus!*"

"Don't blaspheme." She looks at me. "Anyhow, *he* would-
n't keep quiet . . ."

"We *go*," Father says.

Mother washed Nickie's hair and put it up in curlers.
When it was dry she brushed it for about a hundred hours. I
hate it when Mother brushes Nickie's hair, because that's
when she tells about the Kings of Ireland and she makes me
listen, too, or at least sit there. She tells about those Kings that
she and Nickie are related to, who could read and write when
the French were still savages, tells all their names, and then
about some little people who give you your wishes. I wish I
could go outdoors but I have to wait till she gets out the
picture of the Lakes of Killarney for her and Nickie to look
at.

When the brushing and the Kings of Ireland were finally
over, Mother got the pink silk dress she'd made and helped
Nickie put it on. "Little princess," Mother said. Mother put
on a new dress and a new sweater. Blue like her eyes. She
looked pretty, and her eyes were shining. She put on her string
of little white beads that Nickie says are real and will be *hers*
when she's eighteen. Mother washed my ears and my neck
and combed my hair till my head hurt. I had to put on my
winter pants because my summer ones are too worn out. I
put on a new striped jersey Father brought me. He put on
extra hair oil and a white shirt and black silk socks with yellow stitches up the sides and his best suit.

It wasn't so bad. The new people changed Mrs. Bradford's
house around so much that she wouldn't know it. Probably it
looks nicer. Father looked and then said to Mother, "You
see? It was mistake to build new 'ouse. Old 'ouse, she is
better." Mother said, "Draughty," but it was warm. I liked
looking at the shape of that shiny black piano. On top of it
was one of the black cases, and in a way its shape was like
the piano's shape. Mrs. Ambler was there, and the Ballatos
from down the road, and a lot of people I never saw before.
In one of those cases was a violin. It was even better to look
at than the piano.

Then they played music. When I got tired of listening I went to sleep on Father's lap. Next thing I knew we were outside in the moonlight and Father was carrying me to the car. *She* came up, her hair looked silver in the moonlight. She put one finger on my cheek and said, "He got through it very well, didn't he?" and Father laughed, and she said, "Come again, Jean-Louis," meaning me. I went to sleep in the car and don't remember going up to my room. Nickie says I missed a lot of good rich food at the end of the party.

All morning it was raining so I drew violins up in my new room where Nickie can't come. Then the sun came out and sparkled all over the raindrops. "Come on, Champion." We went out. We ran right down to Mrs. Bradford's house. The strange-looking car was still there but the front door was shut and the bedroom shutters were closed. I watched and watched but there was nothing to see. On the way home I found a bird's-nest lying on the ground. It has three blue eggs and some feathers in it. I put it away with my other things.

After lunch Nickie put on her second-best dress and took off her hair-curlers and said to me, "Go and wash and put on a clean jersey so we can pay our party-call." First we went outside and picked a lot of Mother's flowers. Mother was over at Mrs. Ambler's and didn't know. We made two bouquets. Nickie's was all blue and white. I made mine yellow and gold out of marigolds and poppies. Nickie tied them both up nice and tight. Then Champion and I and Nickie ran down the hill. The car was gone and the shutters were open. *She* was sitting outside in a long chair with a foot rest at the bottom of it. We stood by the fence. Pretty soon she opened her eyes and saw us. "Hi," she said. "Come on in." We stood on the grass and she sat on her chair. "That's a very large dog," she said.

"This is my dog Champion," I said, "and he hasn't even got his full growth yet because he's still a puppy."

"My," she said and opened her eyes very wide. Her eyes are not brown like Father's and mine, but more like the color of her hair, with darker dots in them.

We gave her our bouquets and she liked them. "Let's have tea," she said. We followed her into the house. The kitchen was full of dirty glasses and plates from last night. She didn't even look at them. She found two glass bowls and put our bouquets in water. Then she made the tea. "We'll use the *French* china," she said. Nickie helped her set the teatray. Champion and I looked around at everything and he cleaned off a couple of dirty plates. "Let's go in the other room," she said. In there everything was in a mess too. Dirty ashtrays and more of those dirty dishes. Only the piano was clean and shiny, with just that one violin case sitting on it. "Well, make some room someplace," she said.

When she said tea I thought she meant some white water that gets colored brown from little bags, and milk for Nickie and me, the way we have it at home when the priest comes. But it wasn't like that. We all had the same thing which was pale green in very thin grey cups. "I'd rather have milk," I said. Nickie kicked my ankle and said, "He's only joking." Anyhow, the chocolate cake was good.

"I'll help you clean up," Nickie said to her.

"You couldn't do that, dear. It's much too much."

"I do the dishes all the time at home," Nickie said. I could have said this was a lie: Nickie only does the supper dishes after Mother gets mad or else bribes her with a quarter.

"I'm trying to get a cleaning woman, but no luck yet."

"Oh you'll never get anybody here in the *backwoods*," Nickie said.

"It's not," I said. "It's the country."

"That's what I think," she said, "and perfectly beautiful it is, too." But she squeezed Nickie's hand to make up for disagreeing with her.

We all got up and went out in the kitchen again and cleaned up for hours and *hours*. Champion was bored stiff.

"Well, Nickie," she said, "you've saved the day. I wish I could do something for you. Maybe you'll think of something."

"Come *on*," I said. "Champion wants to go out."

She went right back to that long chair and put her feet up.

"Now, tell me about yourselves," she said.

"You can catch a lot of trout off the bridge right down there," I said. "At least, my father can."

"That's not what she means, silly."

Then Nickie began telling her about school, and about who lives where, and how Father works the rock-crusher at the quarry and how Mother used to live in New York City. *She* kept Nickie going with her questions. They sounded like Mother and Mrs. Ambler when they get going on the telephone. Champion went off on a run in the woods behind the house. I went around looking under stones for snakes or toads. I didn't find any. I found a pile of old shingles. I picked out a good one and went back to where her chair was and sat down on the grass. I got out my new clasp-knife. I decided I would make her face — the way I'd seen it last night before I fell asleep.

"It was a *romance*," Nickie was saying. She flopped herself down on the foot rest part of that chair. "Father was in the Free French Navy and his ship was in New York. He and a friend of his came ashore and went to a restaurant to have dinner. Father had on his blue uniform and all his decorations . . ."

"We have the uniform home. You want to see it?"

"If your father wants me to. Go on, Nickie."

"When they got in the restaurant they couldn't order their dinner because nobody could understand them. But mother was in there with some of her girl friends. Right at the next table. So she helped them."

"Your mother could speak French?"

"She *taught* French. In a school in the Bronx."

"Then?"

"Then she and Father fell in love. In five days his ship sailed, he went back to the war—"

"He was blown up three more times," I said. I jumped

up and ran all around them doing duh-duh-duh-duh-*duh* like a machine gun.

"Hush, Jean-Louis. Sit down."

"It wasn't like *that*, anyhow," Nickie said. "It was more like *boom*." I sat down and picked up my shingle again.

"Go on, Nickie."

"Then he came back like he promised and Mother had waited like she promised. And they got married."

"Well," she said. "Well. From *l'Île d'Oleron* to Stonecrop. Quite an Odyssey."

I didn't know what she was talking about except that she was saying the name of Father's place just like he does.

"And from the Free French Navy to the limestone quarry," she said.

"No," Nickie said. "First they lived in the Bronx with Auntie Loretta and my grandmother O'Reilly that's dead now and Father worked in a bakery. I was born there," Nickie said, as she's always telling *me*. "But Father didn't like it there. He didn't like the Bronx or New York City or working all night as a baker. He said if he wasn't going back in the Navy, he was going to live in the country."

"Very brave," she said.

"Was it? Mother says it's very lonely. But Father says you have to raise your family in the country."

Champion came and pushed my arm with his paw. "Aren't we ever going to *do* anything?"

"What would you like to do, Jean-Louis?"

"Go fishing." I threw down the piece of shingle and closed my knife and put it in my pocket.

She picked it up, that piece of shingle. She looked and looked. "May I keep this?"

"I don't care."

"We have to go home now," Nickie said.

"No, we don't," I said.

Nickie pinched my arm. "He's just a boy, he doesn't know what's polite."

She looked at that old shingle again. "That's not really

important," she said.

"Well, thanks for the tea," Nickie said.

"I hope you'll come again," she said.

"Thank you, I'd like to, Mrs. Marcus," Nickie said.

"Oh, call me Judy," she said. "that's my name." She kissed Nickie goodbye. "And you, Jean-Louis? Are you coming again?"

"Sure," I said. "I'm coming every day."

Since Judy came to live in Mrs. Bradford's cottage, we're busy. A lot busier than going to school. Every morning as soon as breakfast is over and Judy's husband's gone to the Music Center with his second-best violin, we run down the hill. Nickie washes all the dishes and makes the beds and dusts. She gets one dollar every single day for this and she is saving up for buying a dress from the catalogue, for some Christmas party or something, every dime of it. She won't even buy us a chocolate bar. While Nickie does her work, Judy and I do ours. Judy plays on her piano and I draw. Champion waits outside. Next, Nickie gets her piano lesson. It sounds awful so I go outside, too. Champion and I usually take a run up the mountain or back into the woods. Champion catches rabbits sometimes and brings them back to Judy but she doesn't like them any better than Mother does, even though they're practically whole. If it's raining he comes into the woodshed with me and I carve things. Sometimes Judy buys those pieces of wood or my drawings. She gives me a quarter apiece. Nickie said why should I get paid — "*I* do the work," she said, "he doesn't."

"An artist is worthy of his hire. Even though he seldom gets it . . ."

"So there, Nickie."

"Hush, Jean-Louis."

Father is saving up his quarters and now I am saving mine. He's going to buy a new gun. I'm going to buy a gun too. Father says his twenty-two isn't good for anything but bluejays, and this fall he's going up the mountain and shoot us a deer. We'll have venison all winter and Mother won't spend so much at the store. With my gun I'm going to squirt Nickie when she pinches me, and that old Mrs. Bradford if she comes back and takes the cottage away from Judy. Only I can't save enough quarters because I have to buy chocolate bars and Mother's birthday present and sometimes crayons or paper if Judy forgets them. Only pretty soon I won't need crayons so much because Judy's giving me watercolor paints.

After they get through with that awful piano lesson it's time for lunch. Usually we have lunch with Judy. It's not the same kind of lunch we get at home or even at school. Judy says she never ate a frankfurter or a peanut butter sandwich in her life and she isn't going to start now. But I like her food, even if I don't know what it is exactly. Sometimes we have to have lunch at home because Mother says we "mustn't impose". But not very often because Mother goes over to Mrs. Ambler's house every morning now to look at the baby and watch television and she forgets the time.

Once Mother came to lunch at Judy's with us. She got all dressed up, in the clothes she wore the night of the music. Judy only had on her yellow gardening pants because we were weeding her flowerbeds. I thought Mother and Judy were going to talk about the Bronx and Mother would have a friend from the city, but Judy hasn't ever been in the Bronx and they didn't seem to have much to talk about, after all. So Judy asked Nickie to play a piece on the piano and Nickie did and Mother liked that. Then Judy tried to talk to Mother about my crayon pictures, but Mother said, "His teacher at school says he can't draw." So Judy didn't say any more and quite soon we went home and left Judy there alone.

Now the only times we all see each other is when Father goes fishing. Judy comes to watch and sometimes her husband, too, if he hasn't got a headache when he comes home from the Music Center. Father always says they should come and spend the evening with us, but Mother never says anything.

Once a week Judy and I give Champion a bath so he

won't be a smelly dog. That is, I cover him with soap and Judy hoses it off and I get all wet. While we wash Champion Nickie goes to visit Mrs. Ambler's baby, so Mrs. Ambler's feelings won't get hurt. One day, after a visit, Nickie asked Judy why *she* didn't have any baby. Judy's face got all pink. She pointed at the best violin, in its case on the piano, and said, "*That's* our baby," and looked like she would cry. But she didn't. She stroked Nickie's hair and mussed mine up. She said, "You are both very good friends of mine."

One day when it was time for Champion's bath, Nickie didn't go to Mrs. Ambler's. She hung around interfering. When I told her to get out of our way, she pinched me. So I kicked her shin. She kicked back. I hit her in the stomach. Then I was wet all over — Judy turned the hose on me. She was mad. "Go in the woodshed, Jean-Louis, and dry off. And *cool* off." She took Nickie in the house. Champion ran up the mountain. I went in the woodshed. Judy keeps old bath towels in there for me. When I was pretty dry I went to the front door. She was giving Nickie what for. So I went in the house. Judy gave *me* what for. "Don't you know you're not to hit people, especially women?"

"Father does," I said.

"I'll tell Mother you told," Nickie said.

"Of course," Judy said, "if you're a tattle-tale, Nickie, it's no wonder he *wants* to hit you." She was still mad, all right. "But that doesn't mean you *can*, Jean-Louis."

"Father does," I said again.

"Don't stick your lower lip out at *me*, you naughty Frenchman! As for your father — well, he went to fight with the *maquis* when he was only fourteen years old and, after that, with the Free French Navy, besides being blown up three times—"

"Four times, I said.

"Four times. So you have to make allowances."

"Is the *maquis* the Resistance?" Nickie asked.

"Didn't your father tell you that?"

"I don't remember," Nickie said. "Anyhow, how do you

know that? About the Resistance? We never told you that part yet."

"Because my brother was in it, too. He knows about your father. Everybody knew about your father." Judy smiled at Nickie. "You see, you're related to a hero of the French Republic!"

"*I'm* not French," Nickie said. "I'm descended from the Kings of Ireland."

I made a loud groan and Judy told me to hush. "What you both are," Judy said, "is Americans. But also you are both French and both Irish. Might as well make the best of it." She laughed. What's funny about those Kings of Ireland, I'd like to know?

When Nickie and I went home Mother started scolding about my wet clothes and my muddy shoes, and Nickie said, "You have to make allowances."

Every Saturday morning we get up early and get down the hill in good time so Judy's husband won't get nervous and we go up to the Music Center where the Orchestra plays and listen to a rehearsal. Judy's husband is sitting right beside the conductor and has his best violin with him. We sit in the front row. At first only Nickie could go because Judy thought I'd get tired. I guess she thought I'd make noise or run around. But now I go too because I promised to be quiet. There are more people playing than there were that night at Judy's house, and more kinds of things to play on. There are all those violins and bigger and bigger violins. You can draw them like a family. Then there are things to blow on in different ways, especially some very good shiny brass ones. There is a man busy with a lot of drums. When he isn't hitting them, he's fussing with them. There's plenty to draw there and Judy lets me, because then she's *sure* I'll be quiet. She's taught Nickie the names of every one of those things that get played. As soon as I save up enough I'm going to get me a trumpet. You couldn't hear somebody practicing on the piano through that.

Mother and Father don't come to the rehearsals. They go every Saturday night, by themselves, with tickets Judy gives them, to the real concert. Nickie was supposed to get a quarter for baby-sitting, but as I am no baby any more I said that wasn't fair. So we each get a quarter for sitting with each other. After the concert, in what Mother says is the dead of night, Judy and her husband have a party down at the cottage. If I wake up I can look down and see lights and cars and hear music and people's voices talking and laughing. Sometimes Father goes to these parties but Mother doesn't. She says she can't eat or drink anything after midnight on a Saturday because of going to mass on Sunday. "Why can Father go to a party, then?" I asked her. "Because he's *fallen away*," Mother said. What is that, I wonder. But from the look I see on her face I decide not to ask her.

Sometimes on Saturdays, after our supper is over, but before it's time for the concert, I go out. I say I'm going to take Champion up our hill. But I don't. I sneak down to Judy's house and watch her leave for the concert. Since she came to live in Stonecrop she looks different. Her skin is all sunny. That is, her face and her shoulders and her arms and her legs are now the same color as her hair. When she's dressed up for the concert she wears sun-colored clothes, made out of lace or miles of thin cloudy stuff, and on cold nights a piece of fur the same color — so that she is gold all over from head to foot. I and Champion squat in the bushes by the fence and we see her come out carrying the best violin case and get in the car. Her husband comes out and gets in and they drive away. Then I go home.

IV
Autumn

Summer goes away fast. All of a sudden the concerts were over. We went up to the Music Center with Judy. Nobody else was there. Leaves were starting to turn and some were blowing away and landing on the grass around the Hall. The Hall was closed up. Judy shivered. "It gets cold early here," she said,

"It's *warm*," Nickie said. Judy said that she hates winter. "It's only fall now," Nickie said.

"Even in the warmer climate where I was born, winter was long," Judy said. "Only once, in Switzerland, it was good."

We told her we like winter. "You ought to stay here," Nickie said, "then you'd see how good it is. We have a sled. And we made a snowman last year."

"I could bring Champion down to see you every day after school," I said. "And you can ride on our sled too."

Judy said she has to go to Boston this winter with her husband. But she says maybe she'll come back for Christmas, so she can go she-ing. "What's that?" we asked her. "It's like going on the sled only better," she said. We told her nothing is better than the sled. She laughed and said, "You'll see. In the meantime, though, Alec and I are going to spend our vacation right here. Now. A whole month."

"What about Mrs. Bradford?" Nickie said

"We've rented the place for one more year. So we'll have it for Christmas, perhaps, and certainly we'll stay in it next summer." Then Judy said maybe she will buy that cottage.

"Hurray! No more nasty old Bradford!" I ran all over the grass and kicked fallen leaves. Judy and Nickie went to the side of the Hall and when they came back they had those white clothes Judy's husband wears when he plays his best violin.

Now he has gone to Boston for a few days, but she will not be lonely because we go to see her every day; we might even spend the night.

Frost came and killed Mother's dahlias. "Frost the end of August!" Mother said and hugged her own arms. Father put blankets all over the tomatoes and squashes and my bean bushes. Mother says we can freeze in our beds while Father's vegetables keep warm. But she only said that to us. All the maples are turning yellow, orange, red, and colors in between orange and red. On the mountain they look brighter with the pine trees dark between them. Judy and I gather leaves and press them, she mounts them on her paper and I draw them on my paper. Nickie knows how to play a new piece and it doesn't sound as awful as the last one.

I am going to take Judy on a walk and show her my secret place, but I am not going to take her today because we have to go to Afton and buy school clothes. Nickie likes school clothes but I hate them because they make me think how soon we will have to go and sit in that school again.

Our little ducks grew up and Father killed two and pulled the feathers off and gave them to Judy.

Father and Mother went in their room and closed the door and had a talk, not so very loud. When they came out Mother telephoned to Judy and said yes, we would like to come to dinner at her house tomorrow. So we will have Sunday dinner and roast duck, but not until after Sunday school and mass.

Father is all dresssed up in his best socks and shirt and his best suit and a lot of oil on his hair so it will lie down and not be so curly. Mother is dressed up too. She got new things in Afton when we got our school clothes. Father said that caused him to go to the Bank again and he looked mad. Today he doesn't look mad. But after mass Mother looked mad. She said he smelled up the church with his violet hair oil. "If you were not ignorant Irish," Father said, "you would be knowing that it is *French* hair oil." Nickie began to cry in the car and said please woudn't they stop quarreling before we got to Judy's house. Father looked as if he was going to give Nickie one but he didn't, and now we're at Judy's and everybody's smiling at the things she

put at our places on the table. Father's place has his Free
French battleship, small but exactly right. Mother's has little
lakes with trees around them, made out of mirrors and bits
of moss and twigs and pine needles. Mother said, "Killarney!"
and almost cried. Nickie's place has a grand piano cut out
of cardboard and painted shiny. And I have a new kind of
paintbox that isn't watercolors but what Judy says are
gwashes. When everybody gets through ooh-ing and ah-ing,
we can sit down and eat. Mothers oohs the most and then
says, "Where in the world did you ever buy these things?"
and Father gives her a look and says, "She is not buying
them, she is making them herself."

Judy said, "Well, of course I did buy Jean-Louis's paints,
but they didn't cost much."

Then we could eat. The duck was good.

After dinner Judy and Father and Mother had some
French stuff to drink, only Mother had a cup of tea instead,
and Judy talked to them about her piano. Well, first she had
Nickie play the new piece that isn't so awful. Mother
seemed to like it, she smiled at Nickie the whole time. And
Father said, "The girl, she play very nice," and smiled at
Judy. Judy asked what is she going to do with that piano all
winter? — she can't leave it here in a house that will get
damp, and on the other hand how is Nickie going to practice
when Judy's gone? So would Father and Mother do her a
favor and put her piano in our house? (If it's too cold outside, where will I go while Nickie practices?) Father says
it is Judy doing us a favor and *merci mille fois.* Mother says,
"We'll see."

Then it's time to go home. Judy says wait a minute
because there's a surprise for Mother, and I know she means
the leaf pictures I made, but more than that she means the
special drawing.

Just when the music was all finished and the Hall was
empty and the leaves were starting to turn — when we knew
fall was here, that is — Judy asked me to make a picture in
crayons of the summer. At first I acted silly (so she said)

and drew a lot of pictures of boys shooting things with squirt guns and then I lay on the floor and played with Champion. Judy said *"farceur"* and went into the kitchen. After I was tired of rolling on the floor I made a picture. There's a big circus tent, brown, with a dressed-up man, all black and white with a whip, standing outside it calling people to come in. There's another circus tent with no people outside it but it's red and white striped and has a lion beside it. In the very front there's a boy with a flower in his hat standing there and looking at everything. The name of this picture is *Which Circus?* but I couldn't spell that so Judy had to write it. She liked the picture but she didn't give me a quarter for it because she said it was priceless. What did she mean? She didn't say, she asked me what the picture means, so I got silly again and went outside and turned the hose on Champion.

But Mother doesn't want to see that picture. She says, "I'm glad you could keep Johnny out of mischief that way," and we go home.

"Why you no thank that so good Judy for the piano, eh?" Father says.

"Your so good Judy is a so bad flirt," Mother says, "just like you."

"You are wrong," Father says, "but no sense to argue. I only like to know why you no take the piano? Is nice for the girl, no?"

"All right," Mother says, "I'll take the piano if you'll take us to mass every Sunday this winter. Instead of lying in bed like a heretic."

"Priest-ridden Irish!" Father goes in their room and slams the door.

Then it's night and we go to bed. I was asleep but I woke up because of the awful noise. It's Mother and Father in their room making that awful noise. It goes on and on. I get so scared I run down to Nickie's room, and there's Nickie standing in her nightgown and shaking and listening at the wall. Mother and Father are shouting and yelling.

There's a lot of other noise, the same kind as when Father gives me one or gives Nickie one, and noises of things falling down and breaking. Then their door slams and we hear Father walk across the living room. Is he going to break the television set again? Even his footsteps are angry. No, he goes straight out of the house. Going away in the car? We hear the car door slam, but the engine doesn't start. Maybe he's going to make his bed in the car. Mother is in her real bed, we can hear her crying some, then nothing. All quiet, she must be asleep. Our feet are cold and my stomach feels funny. We sneak out of Nickie's room. Champion isn't in front of the fireplace or even under the table. Slugger is behind the cellar door, I see his one eye looking through his cat-hole. Maybe Champion went to keep Father company. Nickie makes us hot cocoa and we sit in the kitchen. We talk about the dress Nickie is going to get from the catalogue with the money she saved and about the toad-houses I am building out of flower-pots. Nickie decides she will not get the dress, she will spend all her dollars on piano lesssons. The cocoa is finished. Nickie says, "You can sleep in my room, even though it's Not Allowed. We won't tell any-body." I don't mind.

Today when we went down to Judy's house so Nickie could wash the dishes and I could draw, Nickie asks, "What are Droits de mon Lit?" in a voice like Father's. I ask Nickie if that's what she heard Father and Mother fighting about but instead of answering she kicks my ankle. Judy says "what?" two times and her cheeks get pink and she says it's a French phrase and is sort of about love. "You mean like we love you, Judy?" Judy says it is in a way but it's for grown-ups and therefore different and then she says we won't draw or wash the dishes, we will go and watch the corn being chopped on Mr. Ambler's field.

Mother has a purple mark under one eye. She didn't go to visit Mrs. Ambler today. She had the priest come over to tea.

Now it is school bus every morning. And Judy's husband

is back from Boston. We run right down to Judy's house when we get off the bus but sometimes Judy can't play with us because she is playing the piano for her husband.

Nickie used to like school. I never liked school. Now she doesn't like it much herself. This morning it was raining. Mother didn't get up. We only had some stuff Father left on the stove for us, a kind of sticky mush. We got wet waiting for the bus. We thought of the warm fire down in Judy's house. Nickie said, "What if we didn't go to school?" She whispered that. I squeezed her hand "yes" and as the bus came along we crouched down in the bushes out of sight, pretending we weren't there. After Fred had honked a few times and finally gone off without us, we were wetter than ever. And we were scared. I wanted to cry. I could just feel Father giving us one, maybe two or three. But I didn't cry. We stood there, wet and not knowing what to do, till Mr. Ballato came by in his pick-up. "You kids miss the school bus?" Nickie crossed her fingers behind her back and said "Yes." He drove us to school.

Now I am glad we did not get into trouble because when Father came home he put us in the car with him and said, "We go to Afton. I buy me now my gun." Mother doesn't have the mark on her face today and since the priest came to tea she is nicer and she came with us. Father has his paycheck (it is Friday, then) and some money from his tobacco jar. He's sharing that with Mother. She and Nickie go to look at dresses. I go with Father to a store only for guns and fishing poles and we see every kind of gun in the world. Father is buying the best one. Soon he will go on the mountain, he says, to shoot him a deer.

Summer was short and we are in what Father calls autumn, which means winter soon. Father says that here only winter is long. But Judy said all winters are long everywhere. Then she locked up her house, she and her husband put all their suitcases and his violins into their car and they drove away. The only bouquets we could find were dried leaves. Judy took them with her. We waved till the car was over the hill and then went home.

Judy's piano looks very big underneath the picture window in our living room. There is nothing to do when we come back from school and Slugger is sick.

Today begins the Game Season, Father says — time for him to go on the mountain. Judy came back! When I went up to my room after school I saw lights shining from her house. Pretty soon she came to our door, with two other people, ones we are to call Aunt Sally and Uncle Otis because they are her brother and sister. Everybody started jumping up and down and laughing and hugging and barking. "We came for the shooting," Judy said. Even Mother was pleased, and when all the laughing and hugging was over, it was decided that we were all eating dinner in our house, cooking steaks over the fire and baking potatoes in the ashes. Father and Uncle Otis talked in French a mile a minute, all excited and with their mouths full. Father kept thumping Judy's brother on the back and saying, *"Mon copain."* I guess Uncle Otis must be the brother that was in that French resistance. Father told me to go get his uniform and everybody looked at the decorations, and then Father told me to put it away so it wouldn't get meat juice on it.

After supper Judy played on the piano, different from her usual music, the kind you can dance to. Father knew all the words to the tunes she was playing and sang them in the French language and so did Judy. Everyone danced — except Judy, of course — even Mother was dancing and after she had some of the kind of drinks everyone else was having, Judy played an Irish tune called a jig and Mother danced it, first alone and then with me, and everyone clapped and Father shouted "Bravo!" Also, Nickie taught me to waltz and never said I was clumsy. When it was time to go to bed, everyone laughed and hugged again. Judy hugged Mother and said, "We'll make *des petites noces* again tomorrow night at my house. Maybe we'll even have some roast pheasant!" And Mother hugged her back and said that would be fine.

Now we are waiting for Father to come home with his deer. I and Nickie and Mother were not allowed to go because it is dangerous. We are keeping the soup hot. Mother says her head aches.

Slugger is lying by the fire all the time and can't get up. Mother says he must go to the vet. Nickie says Judy could drive him there.

We wait and wait. When Father comes in he is very cold. He blows on his red hands and takes the bullets out of his gun. Then he takes off his red cap with the license pinned onto it. We look and look. But there is no deer.

"Me, I am the only one saw any deer," Father says. "They all go the wrong way, the others. I go another way. I climb and climb the damn mountain. I creep and crawl. I lie in the bushes. I get to windward. I lie in more bushes. I am silent. I am free*zing*. Then one comes — ah, she is beautful. I am hide so good she do not know. She come close. I have the gun ready. I point. She come more close. It is like she look at me. I see her eyes, very soft, very brown." Father sat down and took off his boots. "I no can shoot her," he said.

Mother wanted to know why we spent so much money on a gun and now we have no deer. Father answered that he could not say.

It is time for supper at Judy's house. Judy telephones to say that she has some pheasants and they are cooking now. Father says, "*Mon dieu, quelle femme!* She can cook also?" And Mother says we are not going because her head aches and tomorrow is Sunday.

"But tonight, she is Saturday!"

"Not she, it," Mother says.

"Even Irish peasants are not so often thinking of the mass, sure not on Saturday night," Father says.

Nickie says we are not peasants but descended from the Kings of Ireland and Father gives her one on the ear.

I tell him good Frenchmen shouldn't hit girls and he gives me one on the mouth.

Mother puts some cold cuts on the table and turns on

the television set.

Father went to Judy's house alone.

After while it was morning, Sunday morning. Time for Sunday school. I get the usual ear-washing. I have to put on my suit with the long pants that is too big for me. Mother and Nickie are dressed up in the clothes they bought in Afton. They have on hats. Mother has gloves on. She and Nickie have their black boots. We go out to the car. Father is standing by the car. It is dusty from the quarry. He has on his dirty work-clothes from Friday, covered with lime dust. His shirt only has one button and I see his black curly chesthair. He has black whiskers on his chin.

Mother looks and looks at him. Her pink cheeks got red. Finally she says, "Get in, children," and Nickie and I get in the back. She gets in the front. Father gets in his side and starts the car. We drive to Stonecrop without anybody saying one word.

When we get to the church there are a lot of people, all in their Sunday clothes, walking from near by or driving up in clean cars. Father drives up fast and stops short, making noise with the brakes and more dust for the car. Everyone is looking. Father is laughing. He gets out of the car and goes around and opens the door beside Mother and gives a low bow. "*Madame, tu es servie*," he says. He's laughing. Everyone is watching. Mother whispers: "I'll never speak to you again." She gets out and he gives another bow. "I promise I take you every Sunday," he says, "and I am taking you, no? I no promise I come inside." Mother pretends she doesn't hear and motions for us to get out. "I go to mass on Holy Days," he says, "but me, I am French. *Not* priest-ridden. Especially am I *Free* French!"

We went inside the church and Father drove away.

When we came out Father was waiting beside the car. In the meantime he had shaved and put on his best suit and his hair oil. The car was cleaner. Mother pretended she didn't see him. She shoved us in front of her and went to the Amblers' car. "I'd be obliged if you'd give us a lift," she said.

Mr. Ambler was laughing. "That Frenchy! What a card!"

Mother and Nickie got in. I got away and ran over to our car and got in beside Father.

We drove down to Judy's house. Judy came running out — "*Bon jour, bon jour.*" Then she sees all of us aren't here. "Where're your wife and Nickie?" Father starts to tell her about it. They talk in French, very fast, but I know what Father must be saying, because Judy begins to laugh. When he's finished she taps him on the arm and says, "*Farceur!*" Then she stops laughing. "But it's not funny for *her*," she says in English. "You must go home now and make peace. You've had your fun. Now you'll have to eat a little bit of crow."

"Me, I apologize — *jamais!*" Father says.

"Time to learn, Jean-Louis *père*. Free French and all that, it's over. Now it's time for peace."

I can see Uncle Otis and Aunt Sally eating Sunday dinner in there, but Judy does not ask us in, even though Father is dressed in his best clothes. "Off with you!" she says. "*Dépêchez-vous!*"

Father's lower lip sticks out. He starts the car. "Judy! Judy!" I call to her.

She waves. "See you later. Go home and be nice to your mother."

Mother wasn't nice to us. Sunday dinner was some more cold cuts and she didn't eat with us. As soon as we came in she went out. She took Nickie with her. She didn't ask me to come. Nickie looked back at me, maybe wanting me to come, but before I could do anything they were gone. I ran to the kitchen window. "Father, they're going to the Amblers'."

"They can go to *Ell*," Father said.

What if Mother heard *that?*

In about an hour Mr. Ambler came over. "You're in the soup, Frenchy, with the womenfolk." He began to laugh. "They're re-hashing everything and praying all over my

living room. Next thing they'll have the priest onto you.
And you'll be sleeping on your sofa."

"Not me," Father said.

"You're a card, Frenchy." Mr. Ambler has on his hunting jacket and red cap and has his gun under his arm, even
though it is Sunday. "Come on, we'll get us some partridge,"
he said. "I can't stay in my house another minute — and
you might as well be hanged for a sheep as a lamb."

They go out and Champion and I are there with nobody
but Slugger who is sick and lying in front of the fireplace.

"Come on, Champion."

We go down the hill to Judy's house. There's nobody
around. I see firelight inside but no people. Maybe they're
taking naps. I look at the cars. Uncle Otis has a funny car,
too, but different from Judy's. There's a license plate on it
Nickie and I never saw before. There's a long word and then
two letters — "D.C." Now I've seen this one first. I can
claim it. But only Nickie can read all of it, so it will be
a tie. If Nickie ever comes home again.

Pretty soon Judy comes out. She's got on her fur hunting
jacket and a red woolly cap. "I decided to show you my
secret place," I tell her.

We walk down-creek by the road about half a mile. Then
I tell Champion to stay where he is. He's not allowed in the
secret place. "Walk like an Indian, Judy," I tell her, "and
don't talk." We creep through the dead underbrush. Then
we're there. It is my beaver-dam. There are three Canadian
geese resting on the little pond the beavers made. They
don't know we're there yet. People think beavers work all
the time, but I know better. They play. Like now, for
instance. The whole beaver family is playing around in the
water, tumbling and splashing with their big flat tails.
Playing. The geese are so big they don't even notice the
beavers. They have a long ways more to go. They're tired,
they're resting. Then they knew we were there. The geese
rose. Their wings were like thunder. Rising, they were
heavy. When they were in the air they were light as clouds.

They were flying, one in front, then a pair. When we looked down the beavers were out of sight.

We walked back to the road. "Come on, Champion." We walked along the road. We didn't say anything. Judy kept looking at the sky. When we got back to her house she said, "I can never thank you enough, Jean-Louis, for showing me your secret place." Her eyes were running. Maybe she was cold. Her nose looked cold. "And for everything else," she said.

"Can I have supper in your house, Judy?"

"No, dear, because I have to go to Boston, and Sally and Otis have to get back to Washington." She looked at her little watch. I looked at the shadow of the mountain and saw that evening is coming. "Almost right away. But we'll be back for Christmas — all of us, Alec too."

She knelt down on the frozen ground and put her arms around me. "Be my good Frenchman till then," she said. She gave me a big hug. She got up. "Is everything all right at home?"

I said sure, it was. Then she said "*À bientôt*" the way she does and went in her house and closed the door.

V
Departing

Our house was dark. No one was there. Only Slugger. Champion went up and sniffed him, then he went out again. I got my robin's nest with the three eggs and the feathers in it and went outside again. I called Champion but he didn't come. I saw two cars go by and turn onto the Afton Road, going up towards the Turnpike. They didn't see me. I went down the hill and put my robin's nest into Judy's mailbox. That way Judy will have a message from me the first minute she gets back for Christmas.

Coming back up the hill I wished I had Champion with me. It was dark. The bare tree branches were black. Our house with no lights on was black. Maybe Champion went out to meet Father? I do not like our house with no lights inside. But outside it is cold. So I go in and turn on all the lights and the television set and the gas burners on the stove that I'm not allowed to touch. The fire's gone out but Slugger is still lying there. It's cold in the living room. Slugger looks cold too. His eye doesn't seem to see me. I heat up some milk like Mother does for him, except that it gets all over the stove, but when I put the dish down beside him he doesn't drink. I'm hungry. There's a piece of cake in the back of the refrigerator. I eat that and drink milk. I'm still hungry. I eat a peanut butter sandwich. I don't like peanut butter as much as I used to. Why doesn't somebody come home?

Up in my room the moon is shining into my window. It is called a hunter's moon. Maybe Father hunts in the moonlight. But what is Mother doing? I hear the deer belling on the mountain.

I didn't know I was asleep. When I wake up I am very surprised to see that I'm lying on my bed with my clothes on. The moon has set and the sky is getting grey. I wasn't sleeping under my blankets, so I'm cold. I go downstairs. Nickie's room is empty. So is Father and Mother's. Father is in the living room sleeping on the sofa. Slugger is lying in front of the empty fireplace. He looks funny. His eye stares at me. He looks stiff. I touch him and he does not bat me. He's cold too.

I run to the sofa. "Father, Father, wake up! Slugger, he's sick or something."

"Hah?" Father's eyes are sticky. "Jean-*nee*," he says, "it is morning?"

"Father, where are Mother and Nickie? I want my breakfast." I pull him by the hand. "Look at Slugger."

Father gets up sort of stiff. He walks over to the fireplace. "*Il est mort*, poor old cat. Slugger, he is dead," he says. "I throw him in the woods."

"No, Father, no! When Nickie comes home we'll bury him." I'm crying, I guess. I can't help that.

"Nickie, she never coming home," he says. "She and your mother, they at the Amblers'."

Father gets a box from the cellar and puts Slugger in it. Then he goes in the kitchen and puts water and oatmeal on the stove. "Come now, we wash our faces."

Father's wrong about Nickie. While we're in the bathroom she came in. Champion came with her. I run out — "Champion!" — and give him a hug. He doesn't lick me. He sniffs at Slugger's box and howls at the back door, so I have to let him out again. Nickie's new dress is mussed up and her hair isn't curly and she hasn't washed her face at all. She doesn't say one word. Father doesn't either, but he doesn't give her one on the ear.

"Nickie, Slugger's dead." She goes and looks, then she cries some.

It's good Nickie came home because we don't have to eat Father's sticky mush now. Nickie cooks eggs for us and coffee for him, just like Mother does. When Father's through eating, he gets the shovel and goes out and digs a hole in Mother's dahlia bed. "I go to work now," he says when he's finished. "You can bury the old cat. Then you stay home. You both. I come back my lunch hour." He puts his hand on my shoulder and squeezes.

"Mother says she's going away," Nickie tells him.

"She can go. You stay."

"She says she'll take us with her. Like before."

"She do that, I shoot 'er," Father says. "You stay home, you hear me?" Then he looks at Nickie. "You good girl," he says, but she doesn't answer.

Nickie put Champion's breakfast in his dish and I went outside and called and called. But he didn't come.

"Maybe he knows," Nickie said.

"Knows what, Nickie?"

"About Slugger."

"Don't cry any more, Nickie."

"I'm *not*," she said. But she was.

Nickie decided to drink some coffee, seeing she'd made it. I didn't want any because I don't like it. Now Nickie doesn't like it. It made her stomach feel funny.

"Nickie, where's Mother?"

"We stayed at the Amblers'. Mother and I slept in Mr. Ambler's bed and Mr. Ambler slept on the sofa."

"Is that what you mean about going away?"

Nickie shook her head. "No. But maybe we won't have to — Mrs. Ambler says it will *blow over*."

"I wouldn't like to sleep at the Amblers'."

"You didn't have to, did you? I didn't have any room in the bed," Nickie said, "and anyhow I don't like it there. So when Champion woke me up, barking outside the window, I came home."

"I'd rather sleep at Judy's," I said. "But Judy's gone away till Christmas." Nickie said she knew that and that her stomach felt worse.

As soon as Nickie felt better we took Slugger's box outside. I put my dried flowers and my snake's skin and Nickie put her beads from Grandma in the box with him. Then we buried him. We got two thick pieces of wood from Father's workplace in the cellar and I got out my toolbox and nailed them together. Nickie wrote out in big plain letters what I should carve on the cross-piece. "Here lies Slugger. A brave cat. R.I.P.," it says. Even though it's so cold outside that it nips our ears, we get all sweaty pounding that wood into the hard ground.

While we were outside, Mother came home. She and Mrs. Ambler are packing our things. Mrs. Ambler's baby is crying on our living room sofa. Mother is packing her things and my things and Nickie's things. But she is not packing our sled or our new skates or my water color paints or anything important, just our clothes.

"We're going to visit your Auntie Loretta," Mother says.

"*You* can, Mother. But Nickie and I have to stay here."

"You'll spend Christmas with your Auntie Loretta," Mrs. Ambler says. "Won't that be nice?"

"No," Nickie says.

"Christmas? That's a long ways off, Mother, and anyhow we have to be here then because Judy's coming."

"Don't you remember how much you always liked the Bronx?" Mother says to Nickie. "Think of all the lovely shops full of Christmas toys . . ."

"I *don't* remember," Nickie says. "I only pretended to. And I don't want to go. I'm going to stay here."

Two cars drive up. One is the priest's and the other is the taxicab from Afton. Mother cries all over Mrs. Ambler's neck. "There, there," Mrs. Ambler says, "it'll come out all right, you'll see. He'll come and get you, like he did the other time. Then things'll be better. You'll see."

Mother hollers something into Mrs. Ambler's neck that sounds like, "I don't want him," and Mrs. Ambler says Mother mustn't say such things and she goes and picks up her baby that's howling on our sofa and the priest comes in. The priest tells Mother that what she's doing is *wrong*. Nickie runs to the priest and cries. I run to the back door but the taxicab man is standing there and Mother says, "Stop him!" and the man grabs me by the collar of my snowsuit and I can't get away.

It was all so fast I don't know how it happened. In about one minute Mother and Nickie and I were in the back seat of that taxicab with Mother hanging onto both of us very hard, and our suitcases were in the front seat with the driver, the doors were shut and we were driving out into Bradford Road, with Mrs. Ambler in our driveway waving and the priest standing beside her shaking his head and then we'd turned into the Afton Road and were tearing down it in that taxicab. With the trees bare for winter I could see our house from that road. I was looking back at it and I saw Champion come out of the woods. He ran out to the Afton Road and tried to catch up with the taxicab but he couldn't.

I saw our house get smaller and smaller, but the mountain behind the creek, with the snow on top of it, was still big.

Jim Brooke

TEO SAVORY's novels reflect the diversity of places in which she has lived and of the careers pursued before she turned to writing and editing. Her first book, published in New York, takes place in China; the second, THE SINGLE SECRET (Braziller, New York/Gollancz, London) is laid in her now familiar territory, the fictitious village of Stonecrop in a district —Afton County—"somewhere in Western New England." Her next novel (A PENNY FOR THE GUY, Gollancz, published here as A PENNY FOR HIS POCKET) switches to wartime London, with a brief interval in Hollywood; then, in TO A HIGH PLACE (Unicorn), further back in time to the England of the early years of this century and ending in China and Tibet. In STONECROP: THE COUNTRY I REMEMBER (Unicorn, 1977), the author returns, with the "authenticity only a master storyteller could evoke" *(Booklist),* to her imaginary Afton County, which is also the setting for her most recent publication, the novella, A CHILDHOOD. In between, Miss Savory has had published her collection of short satirical prose, A CLUTCH OF FABLES (Unicorn, 1977)), four poetry sequences, and fourteen books of translations from French, German and Vietnamese. In personal terms, then, Teo Savory was born in Hong Kong, educated in London where she lived and worked for several years before she moved to New York and became involved in theatrical production. She began writing when she moved to Western Massachusetts which is now her home for part of every year.

COLOPHON

A CHILDHOOD by Teo Savory was typeset at Types Inc. of Greensboro in 11 pt Janson linotype. The book was printed and bound by Edwards Brothers Inc. of Ann Arbor. Alan Brilliant designed the book and handset the titling.